Rachel

Emily and Emerald

Kelly McKain

THIS DIARY BELONGS TO

Emily xxx

Dear Riders,

A warm welcome to Sunnyside Stables!

Sunnyside is our home and for the next week it will be yours, too! My husband Johnny and I have two children, Millie and James, plus two dogs … and all the ponies, of course!

We have friendly yard staff and a very talented instructor, Sally, to help you get the most out of your week. If you have any worries or questions about anything at all, just ask. We're here to help, and we want your holiday to be as enjoyable as possible – so don't be shy!

As you know, you will have a pony to look after as your own for the week. Your pony can't wait to meet you and start having fun! During your stay, you'll be caring for your pony, improving your riding, learning new skills and making new friends. Add swimming, games, films, nature trails and a gymkhana and you're in for a fun-filled holiday to remember!

This special Pony Camp Diary is for you to fill with your holiday memories. We hope you'll write all about your adventures here at Sunnyside Stables – because we know you're going to have lots!

Wishing you a wonderful time with us!

Jody xx

Monday — I can't believe I'm really here at Pony Camp!

I feel EXCITED about being here, but NERVOUS at the same time!

I'm EXCITED 'cos I haven't ridden since we moved down here from London three weeks ago – I can't wait to get back in the saddle! And I'm NERVOUS because at the stables where I used to ride and help out at weekends there were these older girls and … well, I don't really want to write all about what happened with them in my lovely new Pony Camp Diary. And, anyway, this is meant to be a new beginning.

Actually, me and Mum are both having a fresh start down here in Dorset. As it's the summer holidays I haven't started my new school yet, so it's been a bit boring 'cos I've just been helping Mum unpack boxes and paint the living room.

I felt extra NERVOUS when Jody showed us up here to my room. I wanted Mum to stay for a while, but she had to go back to the new house and wait for the gasman, so I ended up on my own. There are three beds in here, and Jody said the one by the window was her daughter Millie's, so I had the choice out of the bunk beds. I went for the bottom one, and as I started unpacking my stuff, I could hear all this noise and laughter coming from the room next door.

The two girls in there were really loud and confident – the exact opposite of ME! Then I heard all these footsteps on the stairs and someone yelling, "Hey, Harry!" at the top of their voice. For about one second I thought there was a BOY at Pony Camp, but then I heard this girl's voice yelling back and I realized that Harry must be short for Harriet.

And that was when Frankie bustled in with her mum, who is also really loud and who kept on calling her Francesca. I felt really shy and I wished I could shrink into a corner and disappear. But when Frankie rolled her eyes at me, I couldn't help smiling. She shooed her mum out and said hello, and after a few seconds of me blushing shyly with no words coming out I finally managed to mumble, "Hi, I'm Emily."

Frankie said, "Hi, Ems. Call me Frankie, everyone does. Well, apart from *her*, of course!"

She waved towards the door, obviously
meaning her mum. "And my big sister Harry
when she's trying to annoy me! That's her loud
voice you can hear, by the way – she's got such
a big mouth!"

I smiled as she threw her stuff on the top
bunk. No one's ever called me Ems before –
I quite like it. I was trying to think of something
to say when Harry put her head round the
door and shouted, "Come on, Frog Face, we're
all going down to the yard!" She grabbed

Frankie's arm and started pulling her out of the room. Frankie giggled and cried, "Don't call me Frog Face, Monkey Breath!" Then Frankie tried to grab my arm, and I wanted to go with them, but my feet stayed stuck to the spot. For some reason, I don't seem to be that good at joining in.

"I'll be down in a sec!" I told them, as brightly as I could. "I just want to start off my diary first."

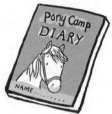

So that's what I've been doing!

Oh, hang on, even the other room with the younger girls in has gone quiet so everyone must be outside. Right, I'm going to take a deep breath and put on my hat and body protector (and a big smile), and go down to the yard.

Monday 1.45p.m. — well, I still can't believe what happened this morning!

I'm so EXCITED and NERVOUS again! EXCITED because I have met the most amazing pony called Emerald, who I'm desperate to have as my own for the week. And NERVOUS because I'm waiting to hear from Sally, our instructor, about whether I can have her or not.

Sally's gone off to speak to Johnny about it (he's the yard manager and also Millie's dad), and she said she'll come and find me after lunch. We've finished eating now, and I'm writing this sitting at the picnic table outside the farmhouse so I can keep a lookout for her.

OK, well, this is a pic of (fingers crossed!) my fab pony, Emerald!

She isn't supposed to be one of the Pony Camp ponies at all, but as soon as I saw her I knew I wanted her, and Sally did admit it seems like Emerald has chosen me, too. But she also said I'd have to ride Flame first in the assessment and, oh whoops, I'm trying to say everything at once and missing things out. Right, I'll take a deep breath and slow down and write everything in order.

OK, so I headed over to the yard to find the others, and as I walked between the car park and lower field this pony came bolting towards me, completely loose, with a head collar on and her lead rope dangling. It was Emerald! I didn't know her name then, of course. And I didn't know that she'd just arrived at Sunnyside and had gone bombing out of the trailer as Sally was unloading her. But I did know that she was the most gorgeous pony I'd ever seen.

She was skittering around, looking ever so frightened. For a moment I froze in shock, but then I thought how dangerous that dangling lead rope was, and how I had to stop her from tripping up and having an accident.

I stood my ground as she came right up to me, and I spread my arms out so that she couldn't get past and gallop off up the track to the upper fields.

I took a deep breath and tried to relax. Emerald lowered her head and snorted; she seemed to be calming down a bit, too. I stepped towards her and put my hand out for her to smell.

"Be careful!" Sally called, as she appeared round the corner. I gave a slight nod, then slowly turned so I was standing at Emerald's shoulder, and reached down for the end of the lead rope.

Then I stood there with both hands on the rope while Sally came over and took it from me. "Well done!" she said softly. "You showed a lot of horse sense by staying so calm."

I smiled, and inside I was really proud of myself.

She asked my name, and just when I thought she was going to send me off to the yard to join the others she said I could help take Emerald into the barn instead. She told me to lead her into a small pen in the corner, away from the other ponies. As I walked her on, I kept glancing at her gorgeous, glossy bay coat and cute white star and big brown eyes, and thinking how beautiful and special she was.

We got some hay for her and filled up her water trough, and as I was stroking her nose to say goodbye, I blurted out to Sally, "Do you think, maybe, I could have Emerald as my pony this week?"

Sally frowned. "I'm sorry, Emily, but she's not going to be ridden at Pony Camp for a while," she said. "She's very nervous and I need to work with her myself first."

I tried to smile, but I couldn't hide how disappointed I was. Emerald leaned her head over the railing and nudged my arm. I rubbed her neck and she snorted gently.

"It wouldn't be an easy week," Sally said then. I stared at her. Was she saying yes after all? "I've ridden Emerald myself and I know her temperament and capabilities," she continued. "You won't be able to jump her, and you'll have to keep her calm in flat work or she might bolt off with you."

"I don't mind," I insisted. "I don't care about any of that, I just want to be with Emerald."

Sally smiled. "I know you do, Emily, but we have to be sensible. I'll need you to ride another pony in the assessment lesson, so I can see what level you're at. And then we'll think about it. OK?"

"OK!" I cried, grinning.

So I gave Emerald a last pat, and showed her that I had my fingers crossed for us. Then Sally and I went to join the others, who were all hanging around outside the office, squished on to the bench and chatting away. I hung back behind Sally as we neared them. I wish I could just talk to new people like that, as if I've known them for ages. Frankie and the others make it look so easy.

Everyone had already introduced themselves, but Sally got them to say their names to me, too, which made me the centre of attention and left me feeling completely embarrassed!

The other girls are:

Frankie Morgan Harriet Neema Elena Madison Chantelle Millie

Harriet said she and Chantelle and Elena (she's Spanish so you say it as Elay-na) are all 12 and in the same class at school. They're sharing

a room in the farmhouse, too. Madison and
Morgan are 8 and 9, and they've come all the
way over from New York. They're staying with
their English grandma for the summer, and she
had the idea of sending them to Pony Camp. I
just love their American accents! They're sharing
the other room with Neema, who's only-just-9.
Me and Frankie are both 10-nearly-11 so our
room is the middly-aged one, which we're
sharing with Millie.

The girls all seemed really nice, and as Sally
read out the Safety on the Yard rules I wished
I could just pile on to the bench, too, but I
stayed put. I didn't quite dare join in with
everyone, in case one of them shoved me off.
Maybe that sounds a bit of a strange thing to
say, but the older girls at my last yard seemed
nice at first, too, and they turned out to be
really horrible, so I can't help thinking that
kind of stuff.

Luckily, everyone had to get up then 'cos we were going on a tour around Sunnyside. We found out about the fire drill meeting points, and we were learning the safety stuff as we went round – like in the tack room Sally told us that we must put any brushes or numnahs and things away after using them, and in the yard she showed us how to tie up a pony safely.

As we walked around, everyone was chattering together in a big group, so I just smiled and tried to join in here and there. When Sally showed us the barn everyone went completely crazy over the ponies that were being tacked up for us. But I was just gazing at Emerald, who was standing in her little pen, looking back at me.

Then it was time to get matched up with our ponies. Back in the yard, everyone started to pull on their hats and gloves, chatting excitedly. Sally got her list and read out who was on who, as

Sunnyside Stables

Jody and Lydia, the stable girl, led the ponies out.
This is who everyone got:

Emily and Flame

? ? ? ? ?
? ?

Chantelle and Charm

Elena and Jewel

Just for the
assessment. Flame's
lovely, but I really
want Emerald!

Madison and Sugar

Frankie and Star

Morgan and Monsoon

Harriet and Shine

Neema and Prince

Millie and Tally
(her own pony!)

We all mounted up and rode out into the manège. As we began walking round the track, with Chantelle and Charm leading the way, I sat up nicely on Flame and tried to concentrate on riding really well, to prove to Sally that I'm good enough to handle Emerald.

When we'd walked round on both reins and done a few circles and walk to halt transitions, Sally called out for each of us to trot to the back of the ride in turn. When it was my go, Flame had a little buck and skitter and went sideways, and she wouldn't go into trot. I got a bit flustered in case Sally thought I was rubbish for not making a nice transition, but then I made myself take a deep breath, get down into my seat and steer Flame back on to the track. I took half the long side to get a really forward-going bouncy walk so that when I asked again she trotted on without messing around. And it worked!

"Good girl, Emily!"
Sally called out.

"Yeah, go, Ems!"
whooped Frankie.

"Erm, excuse me,
who's the teacher here?"
said Sally sternly, but she wasn't really cross.

Frankie giggled and I couldn't help smiling,
too. I think maybe she is a really truly nice girl
and not just nice to you when she feels like it.

The rest of the lesson went quite well,
although Flame had a bit of a freak-out when
I asked for canter. But I kept calm and asked
again in the next corner, and then we got it OK.

After the assessment, I was worried about
not doing everything perfectly on Flame, but
Sally smiled at me on the way back to the yard.
She said *she* was impressed, but she just had to
go and speak to Johnny…

Oh, there she is…

Two mins later –
I CAN ride Emerald!!!

I'm writing down Sally's exact words so I can remember them FOR EVER.

She said,

"Flame really tested you today, and you kept calm and in control. You're not just a good rider, Emily, you've got a really good understanding of ponies, too. I think you'll be OK to have Emerald as your pony this week."

Well, something like that, anyway!

I nearly hugged her, but I didn't because she is the instructor. I couldn't stop beaming, though!

Gotta go – it's time to get down to the yard. I can't wait to see my GORGEOUS pony!

MY pony – hee hee.

I can't believe she's really mine.

Monday, after our second lesson

I'm so happy that I got to ride Emerald this afternoon! But the lesson didn't exactly go very well. After lunch, we gathered in the yard and Sally read out which groups everyone would be in. They are:

Group B (my group)

Chantelle and Charm

Elena and Jewel

Harriet and Shine

Millie and Tally

✳ Emily and Emerald ✳

Group A

Morgan and Monsoon

Madison and Sugar

Neema and Prince

Frankie and Star

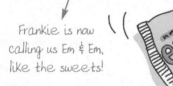

Frankie is now calling us Em & Em, like the sweets!

Sally explained that she'll see how Emerald gets on in Group B, but that we might have to go into Group A for some lessons – like if my group's doing jumping, because she doesn't think Emerald would be able to cope with that.

I said that was fine, and it was so lovely how Frankie grabbed my arm and said, "I hope you do come into Group A sometimes, Ems, 'cos then we can ride together!"

Then we had our lecture about tacking up, so we all got our ponies' stuff out of the tack room to practise on them in the barn. I went straight up to Emerald, staggering under the weight of her saddle, with her bridle jangling on my shoulder, and accidentally gave her a fright. Once I'd calmed her down, Lydia, who was teaching our lecture, called me over to the main pen to join in.

We learnt about the different parts of the
bridle and saddle and what types of bit there
are, and Lydia demonstrated on Prince how to
tack up properly. She also gave us some helpful
tips for the difficult parts like getting the bit in,
and she was really smiley and nice, even when
we got in a muddle.

Then when we had a go for ourselves Sally
came and stood in the main pen with the
others, while Lydia helped me with Emerald.
I'm really glad she did because I didn't want
Emerald to suddenly try and bolt off when
I had the bridle half on.

As we led our ponies out into the yard, I
could tell that Emerald was getting agitated

about being around the others. She kept throwing her head in the air and startling at any tiny noise. I tried to stay calm and not panic, but it was tricky. I love Emerald so much already, and I didn't want to let her down by freaking out. Lydia held my reins for me while I mounted up and got my stirrups sorted out.

As soon as I was on, I found it easy to get a good seat because Emerald is so slim and my legs seem to fit round her in just the right place – see, I knew we were meant to be together!

But in the lesson I couldn't help getting the feeling that she'd rather I was on the floor!

She was just about fine as we walked round the school, although she did keep turning her head too much to the inside. I tried to pull it round, but Sally called out that I should relax

and let Emerald find the bit in her own time.
We were OK doing our walk/halt transitions,
but as soon as we all trotted on as a ride,
Emerald went bucking right across the middle
of the manège to the other side of the track!
Luckily, Sally called out to me to grab the
pommel, otherwise I would've gone flying off.

When Emerald finally stopped, Sally said,
"Are you OK, Emily? Can you bring her back
round past the others and ask for trot again?
We mustn't let her get away with that."

I nodded, although when I took up the reins
again my hands were shaking. I got Emerald to

trot on, but it was a real battle to get her past everyone in a straight line because she wanted to go back over to the other side of the manège. When I finally got to the back of the ride with only one cut corner and two more little bucks, everyone said well done. I felt really embarrassed about them paying so much attention to me, but also quite proud that they thought I'd done OK. Sally said, "Just keep handling Emerald the way you took charge of Flame this morning and you'll be fine."

Emerald is much more of a challenge than Flame, though. We've got so many things to work on! But I hope that once we get used to each other it'll improve.

As I walked her back into the barn to untack, I told her how well she'd done in a soft, gentle voice. After all, she'd tried her best. It's not *her* fault she's so nervous, poor thing! Sally says she came from this old lady who wasn't really well enough to look after her properly and kept her in a little paddock on her own (and *everyone* knows ponies love company). And also that these kids used to go and tease her, chasing her round and trying to get on her.

 THAT MAKES ME SO ANGRY!

How could anyone treat a pony like that?!

At least it can't happen any more. Thank goodness Sunnyside Stables rescued her from being lonely and frightened. But it's not surprising she finds it boisterous and a bit scary here. Poor Emerald! I'll just have to work extra hard at proving to her that she can trust people – starting right now!

It's nearly my turn in the shower, but I said I'd go last so I can quickly write this

Johnny was just about to start our table tennis tournament when Sally poked her head round the games room door and asked if I wanted to help her turn Emerald out for the first time.

Well, of course I did! Any chance to spend more time with my pony!

But it didn't exactly work out in the end.

With Sally beside me, I walked Emerald up the lane to the field. All the other ponies were already grazing, as I led her through the gate and unclipped her lead rope. Then Sally and I leaned on the fence and watched.

Emerald didn't seem to know what to do. At first, she stood by the gate just eyeing the others nervously. Then when Sally encouraged

her to go off, she bolted straight up to Flame,
who just chased her back across the field,
squealing and bucking.

So poor Emerald ended up by herself again.

I felt like shouting to Flame, "Be nice to her!
She doesn't know anyone and she's only trying
to make friends with you!" But Sally explained
that ponies have a sort of special code that new
arrivals have to respect, and that Emerald was
ignoring it.

"Well, she doesn't *mean* to," I grumbled. "It's
not like she's trying to be horrible."

"No, of course not," said Sally. "But she's
been on her own for so long she might have

forgotten, or perhaps she was taken away from her mother too young, so she never learnt these things in the first place. She doesn't understand how to fit in."

I felt even sorrier for Emerald then. I find it difficult to fit in, too, so I understand exactly how she feels!

Emerald tried to make friends with Flame a couple more times, but she kept getting chased away.

I felt really awful just watching — it reminded me of when Suze at my old yard suddenly decided she didn't like me, and then her friends all followed her lead and wouldn't hang around with me either.

Sally sighed. "This isn't going as well as I'd hoped," she said. "I think we'll have to stable Emerald for a while until she gets the hang of group dynamics."

Of course I wanted my gorgeous pony to join in with the others, but I could see that wasn't going to happen. And we couldn't leave her there feeling frightened and lonely all night. At least in a stable she'd be cosy and safe.

So Sally went into the field and caught her, and we got a nice deep bed ready in a spare stable in the main yard. I led Emerald in, and as I took off her head collar, I gave her a big kiss and cuddle and told her not to worry about the other ponies being meanies because *I* love her LOADS.

I kept finding excuses to stay with her, like filling her water bucket right up, double-checking her hooves for stones and wiping invisible specks of dirt out of her eyes. Sally had to call me away in the end.

When I got back to the games room the table tennis tournament was half over, but I did get to join in the doubles 'cos Frankie asked me to go with her. We turned out to be pretty good against Millie and Neema, and when we won Frankie held up her hand to do a high five.

I did it back even though I was nervous about Chantelle and Harry watching (I thought they might think I was acting like a big head). But they didn't seem bothered.

Oh, that's Millie out of the shower, so I absolutely *have* to go in now, seeing as I'm the last one and I don't want to miss out on having my hot chocolate in the kitchen – yum!

Tuesday — I'm quickly writing this after lunch

This morning when I got on to the yard poor Emerald was hiding at the back of her stable, still really nervous and shy. I made a big fuss of her, and then tied her up outside so I could muck out. While I was giving her a brush down, I had a good talk to her about how brave she was to try making friends with the other ponies last night.

Group B were jumping this morning, so we went in with Group A. Me and Frankie were really happy about being in the same group. First we warmed up in walk and trot and did a few changes of rein and turns and circles to get our ponies listening. Then Jody said we'd practise the gymkhana games we'll be doing on Friday.

Madison and Morgan were really excited because they've never done a gymkhana before. Frankie started telling them all about the different games and how much fun they are, until Jody told her to stop chatting and concentrate on her riding! I've done a couple of gymkhana days, so I know a lot of the games, and also I was feeling quite confident because Emerald had been so good during the warm-up – she even stayed calm when Madi and Sugar trotted to the back of the ride and came to a stop really close behind us.

But when we started practising, Emerald went to pieces. First we had to do the walk, trot, canter game. Me and Frankie went against each other, and she was great – instead of being competitive, she just did the walking up and trotting back really calmly so Emerald wouldn't get razzed up. But even with Frankie and Star completely chilling out, when I asked for canter Emerald bucked and went sideways, nearly running into them.

I tensed up and squealed with fright, and of course that only made Emerald worse, so we had to give up on that game.

When Madi, Morgan and Neema rode against each other, me and Frankie had to stand by the gate. Poor Emerald wasn't keen on those three racing up and down in the same manège as her, and she kept trying to yank the reins out of my hands.

I think she would have been good at the weaving in and out of cones game, if we'd done that first, but she was so wound up by then that

she kept shooting out her hindquarters
when we were bending round the
cones. I did try to hold her in
with my outside leg, but she

ignored it and did her sideways prancing thing.
I got really stressed out then, and I didn't enjoy
the rest of the lesson, especially not when she
bolted off while we were waiting for our go in
the relay race. ARGH!

When we were all untacking in the barn,
Sally came over to me. Emerald was still in her
separate pen, so I was on my own with her.
Sally had noticed it hadn't gone too well, and
I tried to act like everything was fine, but she
could tell I was pretty upset. She even said I
might have to give the gymkhana a miss on
Friday, if things don't improve A LOT.

And then she said the WORST thing, which
was, "Emily, you can always swap back on to

Flame for the rest of the week, if you like. That doesn't mean you won't be able to spend time with Emerald, but you'll get more chance to focus on your own riding and development."

I felt all hot and flustery then, and I really hoped Emerald couldn't understand what she was saying.

I looked at my pony's gorgeous face and stroked her neck. "No thanks, I'm fine," I murmured, hoping Sally wouldn't be too annoyed with me.

"No, I didn't think you'd want to," she said. "I do admire your loyalty and determination. But I'll have to have a think about how we can make this work so that you both get the best out of the week."

"OK," I managed to mutter. "Thanks."

When she'd gone, I gave Emerald a fierce hug. NOTHING is going to separate us!

At lunch, Frankie could tell I was still a bit stressed out and she cheered me up in a typical Frankie-type way, which was by having a competition to see how many grapes we could get in our mouths at once. (I got 9 and she got 12, the big mouth!) We ended up in fits of giggles, and I do feel a bit better now.

12 grapes!

Oh, gotta go. Frankie wants me to go round with her and make a list of everyone's fave songs!

Tuesday before tea,
but after our yard duties

Well, this afternoon Sally rearranged things so
that me and Emerald could have a one to one
lesson with her! So I had the lecture with
Frankie's group (which was really fun, on points
of the horse and colours and conformation),
and then rode in the second manège while they
had their lesson. That meant the Group B girls
had to have their lecture just on their own with
Lydia. I thought they might be annoyed with me
for making things change round, but actually
they were happy 'cos it meant they got to ride
straight away after lunch – phew!

In the manège, Sally asked me to warm up
Emerald by myself, and I felt really grown up
deciding things like when to make transitions into
halt and do turns and circles and go into trot.

After about 15 minutes, Sally called to me to halt at M and she came up and gave Emerald a pat. When she said how well we'd done in the warm-up, I couldn't help grinning with pride, and Emerald looked pretty pleased with herself, too. She definitely prefers being on our own to the group lessons! Then Sally said, "Right then, let's get going. What do you think we need to work on?"

I said:

> I know we need to practise staying on the track in canter, and also Emerald needs to stop leaning on the inside rein when I'm trying to get her to bend on a 20-metre circle, and I've got to stop her shying every time we pass the gate and prancing about in walk, and when she bolts off I have to remember to use half halts and turns to stop her instead of panicking...

I thought I was being really horsey by going into all that detail, but Sally just gave me an amused look. "Actually, there's only one main thing we need to work on," she said, "and it begins with 'c'."

I stared at her, puzzled, and went,  Cantering?

I felt so silly when she said,

 CONFIDENCE!

Of course! If we can both gain confidence, Emerald'll calm down, and then a lot of our problems will improve naturally.

So we got to work. Sally kept reminding me to pay attention to the signals Emerald was giving, so that if she was getting too wound up in walk and threatening to bolt off, I could change direction or circle her or ask for a small section of trot. It was great, but not the kind of thing you can do in a group lesson. Like, you couldn't suddenly change direction without warning everyone!

As the lesson was ending, we had a bit of a disaster, though. Jody opened the gate of the other manège to let Group A out, and when she shut it, it kind of clanged and Emerald went bolting off again and bucked across the manège. I forgot all the confidence stuff we'd been learning and just grabbed the reins and stiffened up.

When Emerald finally came to a stop, my heart was absolutely pounding. It really hit me how much work we still have to do before we'll even be able to fit in with Group A, and I think we can forget about taking part in the gymkhana.

I felt very disheartened, but Sally was quite firm and told me we just have to keep going, one step at a time. Then she got us to do some nice trot and canter transitions on a 20-metre circle, so we'd end on a good note.

Afterwards, I walked Emerald round on a long rein to cool down 'cos we were both boiling! As Sally held the gate for me (being careful not to let it clang!), she said, "We're doing well, but I think I know someone who can help us do even better. How would you feel about missing the carriage-driving trip tomorrow?"

"To be with Emerald?" I asked. Sally nodded and I instantly said it was fine. The more time I can spend with my fab pony the better!

Sally didn't explain any more. Instead she just smiled and said, "OK, let me see what I can arrange. And well done today."

I thanked her, and took Emerald back to her pen to untack and brush her down. As I was a bit late finishing, the Group A girls had untacked already, and Group B were skipping out the barn, chatting away. Then Harry did a really loud laugh at something Elena said and made poor Emerald jump. I stroked her nose and whispered, "It's OK, Em, you don't need to be scared any more. It's different here."

Saying that made me think about myself, too. I'm like Emerald, jumping at every little thing — I'm always expecting the older ones suddenly not to like me. But the fact is that they haven't done anything except be nice.

Then I thought about how Frankie's been such a good friend, and I suddenly realized that I'm starting to trust her, just like Emerald is starting to trust me.

"It really *is* different here, Em," I whispered again. "For both of us."

Wednesday, early in the morning before the others are awake

Last night, me and Frankie made a secret camp by hanging our towels down from her bunk across mine so you couldn't see in. It was so cool! We did try and get Millie to come in with us, too, but she was so fast asleep we couldn't wake her up!

Frankie brought out this big pink tub which was full of yummy things for a midnight feast, and soon we were whispering jokes to each other, and scoffing mini rolls and jelly babies and crisps (we were giggling  so much 'cos we had to suck them instead of crunching so that Jody wouldn't hear us!). It was really fun, like having a sleepover.

I hope Frankie will come for a real sleepover at my new house, like next week or something. I think she will if I ask her 'cos we've become really good friends – *and* she lives in the same town that we've just moved to! In fact, we've got so close that I started telling her something more serious, about what happened in my old yard, with the older girls.

It was *Frankie* who called it bullying.

I hadn't really thought of it like that, but actually she's right.

I told her everything – about how Suze and her friends used to act as if they owned the yard and made me do all the horrible jobs, like poo picking the field and scrubbing the feed and water buckets. And how they did all the nice stuff like grooming the ponies and tacking up ready for people's lessons. And then I told Frankie the worst thing of all – about the way they went quiet when I came into the tack room or wherever, like they'd been talking about me. Then Suze used to say stuff to me like, "Yes, can we help you?" and I always went bright red and wished I could become invisible and melt away. It made me upset even *thinking* about what happened. Frankie put her arm around me then.

"I suppose you think I'm really weedy," I said, but she went, "No way! 'Course I don't think that! I think you were brave to keep going there when they were so awful – it shows how much you love ponies! Anyway, the yard staff should have been keeping an eye out for bullying, and they didn't. That was out of order." She frowned at me and added, "You should've told someone."

I shrugged. Maybe for someone like Frankie that would've been easy, but I'm just so shy.

But I loved that she was so angry with Suze and her mates. She really is a true friend.

Later on, we were talking about schools and we worked out that I'm going to be in the same class as her at Westbrooke Juniors when term starts! Frankie started telling me all about her friends and the different teachers and the lunchtime clubs you can do. Anyway, we completely forgot about being quiet! Frankie started doing an impression of this teacher called Mr Gregson, who's like a  mad scientist, and it made us both laugh so much we had to stuff our fists in our mouths to stop the noise coming out.

Too late, though. The next thing we knew
Jody was coming up the stairs! Frankie vaulted
on to her bunk and scrambled under the
covers. We were both pretending to be asleep,
but we couldn't stop ourselves from giggling
into our pillows. Frankie did this big fake snore
and that made me laugh even more. Jody
hissingly whispered to us to go to sleep, but
she didn't seem *really* angry (phew!).

Oh, it's so cool here at Pony Camp!
Everyone's lovely and I've made a good friend
and got the pony of my dreams! I'm really
looking forward to spending the whole day with
Emerald tomorrow! I wonder what Sally's got
lined up for us? I can't wait to find out!

Wednesday, after the most amazing time!

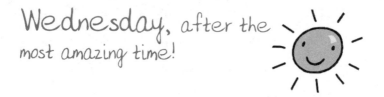

The others aren't back from the carriage-driving trip yet, and I did offer to do extra yard duties in my spare time, but Sally said I'd earned a break. So I went upstairs to get this diary, and now I'm sitting outside in the sunshine, writing! I've had the most amazing day with Emerald. We've both learnt so much — and had loads of fun, too!

Emerald was hiding at the back of her stable when I arrived this morning, but as soon as she saw me she came up for a hug. After the others had set off on the trip, Sally asked me to help Lydia on the yard. Then, about half an hour later, she called me over to the car park.

A dusty old orange pick-up truck, with a wild mustang painted on the bonnet, was pulling up.

My heart was hammering as this huge man climbed out, wearing chaps, a blue checked shirt and a cowboy hat. He looked quite scary from the back, but as soon as he turned round, I knew he was really nice.

Western Bob

He gave me a big smile, then lifted Sally off the ground in a hug and said, "Western Bob at your service, Ma'am." It was funny 'cos he didn't sound American, as I'd expected, but like a normal Dorset person.

First of all, Western Bob asked me to bring Emerald into the manège wearing only her head collar. I'd thought I'd be riding straight away, but Bob said, "We need to get Emerald to trust you, and the best place for that is on the ground."

Bob put Emerald on this really long lead rope, sort of like a lunge rein, and got her to walk round one way and then the other in a circle. Then he let me have a go. My circle was a lot wonkier than his to start with, but after a while Emerald stopped weaving in and out and went steadily round.

We did the same in trot, and then Bob got me to walk around wherever I wanted at the end of the rope and to let Emerald just follow me – I was amazed when she actually did! Then he showed me how to wiggle the rope a bit to get her to go backwards. At first she was confused, but she soon got the hang of it.

Then, when I thought I was finally going to ride, Bob said, "Now, let's give you two a little free time together." I didn't really know what he meant, but then he took the lead rope off Emerald and let her hang out with me in the manège, doing whatever she wanted. And it was so cool that what she wanted to do was follow me around! So we had a walk one way and then the other, and then I tried jogging along and she trotted next to me.

Then she had a trot round and *I* followed *her.* She finished off with a snort and a roll in the woodchips. I didn't copy *that*, of course!

"Good job, Miss Emily,"
Western Bob said, as I
walked back to the gate,
and Sally was smiling loads,
too. She said it was time
for a break then — I felt
really grown up that it was

just me and the two adults, even though they
had coffee and I had orange squash. When Bob
asked me how Pony Camp was going I felt shy
at first, but soon I started chatting away about
Emerald and Frankie and all the other girls and
ponies. I even ended up telling him about our
secret midnight feast!

When it was time to ride, Sally and I gave
Emerald a brush down and tacked up, and soon
I was out in the manège on my gorgeous pony.
And guess what? Sally was riding, too, on her
horse, Blue. She said it would help Emerald get
used to being with other ponies in the manège.

Western Bob had a different style of teaching to Sally. He wanted us to focus on staying relaxed and in tune with our ponies (well, pony and horse!). Like, if they broke out of trot back to walk, we just let them, and then quietly asked them to pick up trot again when they were ready, rather than bothering too much about it. When Sally trotted to the back of the ride and came up behind us, I thought for a moment that Emerald was going to freak out, but she didn't. All that work we'd done on the ground really had paid off!

After about twenty minutes we were nicely warmed up, and Western Bob asked me if there was anything special I wanted to work on. I said, "Not really, I'm just happy if Emerald's happy…" I trailed off, but his smile encouraged me to be brave. "It would be great if Emerald and I could join in the gymkhana on Friday," I said then. "But only if it's the right thing for her."

Western Bob agreed to give it a go, and soon me and Sally were doing the walk, trot, canter race and the weaving through cones one, and Emerald really did enjoy it!

Then Sally said we should make it more realistic, and called to Lydia and her friend Polly to tack up Fly (Lydia's liver chestnut horse) and Rupert, one of the riding school horses. At first, with four of us tearing up and down the manège I really thought Emerald was going to freak out, but she did OK. She got quite razzed up when we were doing the relay race, though, because I had to ride her quite close to Polly and Rupert, but I stayed calm and held her together.

Sally said afterwards how well we'd done, but that in the real gymkhana it will be even more difficult, with people cheering and more ponies in the manège. She said she'd leave it up to me whether we wanted to just do some of the games on Friday, and added that we didn't have to join in at all if I felt that Emerald wouldn't like it. It was great that she was letting me judge for myself what was right for us. It made me feel like we're really a team.

Afterwards, I tied Emerald up in the yard and gave her a proper head-to-hoof groom, and Sally let me wash her tail and then plait it up so it would dry all wavy! Then she came with me while I took Emerald for a walk up and down the lane. I thought we might turn her out

into the field with the other ponies, but Sally
said we should probably leave it one more day.
So my little Emerald is all cosy in her stable
now, tired out and very pleased with herself.
I can't believe how much I love her after only
three days!

I ♥ Emerald!

Oh, the minibus has just pulled up. I hope
the others had a good time – but, urgh, I just
had a horrible thought – what if Frankie has got
really friendly with someone else after today
and she doesn't want to hang around with me
any more? GULP! I really hope not!

Wednesday, after swimming

Well, I was just being silly about Frankie
(phew!). It sounds like they all had a great time
on the carriage-driving trip, though. They each
had a ride in this trap pulled by a pony called
Bayleaf. And they saw all these gorgeous ponies
and horses and different carriages, and they sat
in this really grand one from Victorian times
that's actually been on TV.

It sounded like fun, but I still didn't mind
missing it because I got to spend the day with
Emerald. Frankie said she wished I'd come, but
that she wasn't lonely 'cos she hung around
with her sister and the older girls. Then she said,
"You are coming on the hack tomorrow,
though, aren't you?" And I went, "What hack?"

Frankie said Jody told them about it in the
minibus. Both groups are going together for a

long ride through the countryside, with a picnic lunch halfway. I really want to go and I'm sure Emerald can handle it, so long as I stay calm and focused. But I'll have to see what Sally thinks.

At teatime, all the girls were chattering away about the trip. Because I didn't go I felt kind of left out and I was tempted to just fade away into the background. But something, maybe seeing Emerald's courage in the lessons with Western Bob today, made me try to join in. I asked a few questions, and everyone was really keen to chat to me about it.

Then Elena asked me how *my* day was, and at that moment everyone seemed to have finished talking and they were all paying attention to *me*. I blushed and that old feeling of wanting to turn invisible came back, but then I thought, *If Emerald can be brave, so can I.* And once I started talking about Emerald, I got pulled along with excitement about what we'd done and how much she'd come on today. Then Morgan started telling a story, and I was just sitting there thinking, *Wow, did I actually have everyone listening to me and being really interested?*

That made me feel so happy, and when we went swimming this evening I went and joined in doing handstands on the bottom of the pool and having races and playing water volleyball without even *thinking* that I was joining in. That's amazing for me!

So it's not just Emerald who has gained a lot of confidence with Sally and Western Bob's help. I have, too!

Gotta go, Frankie's saying hurry up 'cos my hot chocolate's getting cold!

Thursday, after our lecture on road safety and first aid and what to do if you get lost (fingers crossed THAT won't happen!)

Sally said me and Emerald can go on the picnic ride with everyone else. YAY! When I went to muck Em out this morning, she was looking out of her stable door, waiting for me! How brilliant is that! I was so pleased and I gave her a massive hug. I started to feel a bit upset then, though, because tomorrow is the last day of Pony Camp. I know that paying for this  holiday was a massive stretch for Mum and there's no way I'll be able to come here for lessons during term time, so it will be the end of Em & Em.

Still, feeling sad made me more determined to enjoy every second I have left with my gorgeous pony. I'm off down to the yard now to tack up, and Lydia's going to show us how to bandage our ponies' legs because we'll be going through the woods and it might be quite brambly.

Sunnyside Stables

Thursday still, but after the picnic ride — well, me and Emerald had the most amazing (and scary!) adventure today

Me and Frankie have worked out that we did about two and a half hours' riding this afternoon — no wonder our legs are so tired! We made sure our ponies had fresh water when we got in and gave them a brush down in the barn, but Sally let us off doing our usual TONS of yard work because we were all so completely flaked out from the long, hot ride. Instead, she let us go swimming to cool off! It was so refreshing diving into the water and splashing about.

So now we've dried off and got dressed, and me and Frankie are writing in our Pony Camp diaries. We're sitting on the platform

71

thing overlooking the manèges (not that there's any riding to watch at the moment, but it's a nice place to hang out).

When we were tacking up our ponies for the ride, Lydia showed us how to put their head collars on under their bridles. I thought it was a bit strange at first, but she explained that while we were having our picnic we could slip the bridles off so they could have a munch on the grass!

Johnny, Sally and Lydia all came with us – Sally was riding Blue and Lydia was on Fly, who is seriously speedy!

We all rode in single file up the road. Sally told me to wedge Emerald in behind Prince and Neema because:

a. Prince wouldn't spook if Emerald jumped at something

and

b. he'd stop her bolting off.

We were all walking along in the sunshine, then we turned up a track and had a little trot and it was just so fab! We rode for ages through some woods and I was a bit worried Emerald would spook at the low branches, but she didn't. In fact, as we walked up this path by the edge of the fields, I was thinking we'd finally cracked it and that she was completely cured of her flighty behaviour – *ha ha, silly me!*

Suddenly, this pheasant flew out of a bush beside Emerald and she totally freaked out.

She went skittering sideways while bucking her legs in the air, and I was so surprised I just fell straight off. I found myself lying on the ground, my heart pounding with shock, listening to her hooves thundering away across the stubble field.

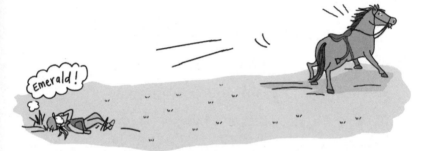

Sally dismounted and handed Blue's reins to someone else (maybe it was Lydia). She crouched beside me and asked if I was OK, but all I could think about was Emerald. I staggered to my feet and went running across the field after her.

"Emily, wait!" Johnny called out, but I heard Sally say, "She won't listen. Don't worry, I'll go." Then she came chasing after me.

When I reached the top of the hill, I saw
Emerald at the far end of the field. She was
pacing up and down with her tail swishing. I
started to run towards her, but Sally caught up
with me. "Go steady," she panted, "or she'll
bolt off. Just get a little nearer, and then wait for
her to come to you."

I blinked at her. I'd been expecting her to tell
me off for ignoring Johnny and then send me
straight back to the group. But instead she was
going to let me try and catch Emerald. I knew
I had to be really slow and careful. If she went
bolting off again, she could run into a road, or
trip up and hurt herself.

I walked down the hill, taking care to stay in
Emerald's sight so I didn't spook her. Then I
stopped, a little way away. She eyed me
suspiciously at first, and shifted from hoof to
hoof. After we'd both stood still for a long time,
I started to worry that she was never going to

come to me. I glanced round and saw everyone standing on the brow of the hill, watching, and I

started panicking that we were holding up the whole ride and that they'd all be annoyed. I think that's why

I tried something stupid. I lunged forward and made a grab for Emerald's rein.

But she whinnied and skittered away.

I felt flustered and frustrated. "Oh, Emerald, come on!" I cried. I didn't want to turn round and look at Sally 'cos I thought she'd tell me off and take over. But I didn't know what to do next.

Then I remembered what Western Bob had taught me.

I couldn't worry about what the others would think. I had to be patient. I had to let Emerald come to *me*.

So I stood, and I stood, and I stood. "It's OK, Em," I said quietly, "you can trust me. And we'll just stay here for as long as you need."

Somehow, Emerald seemed to understand, because after a while she gave me a shy glance, and then another, and then she loped towards me, her neck loose and relaxed. I gave her a big pat and stroke, while gently lifting her reins down over her head. Then I crossed her stirrups over and led her back towards Sally. "I'm so proud of you, Emerald," I whispered.

When we reached the others, Sally gave me a leg-up and off we went again. Instead of being annoyed with me, everyone was chattering about how well I'd done! Of course, me being me, I got embarrassed about being the centre of attention and I couldn't help feeling all red and flustery. But it wasn't in a bad way this time. I didn't want to become invisible. Instead, I felt proud. Of me and of Emerald – Em & Em, the super team! I sat up a little taller and I couldn't help grinning. Now I know Emerald really does trust me, and that together we can achieve anything!

Jody met us at the picnic site in the Land Rover, and handed out sandwiches, fruit and some lovely cold cartons  of orange juice. We clipped the ponies' lead ropes on to their head collars, took the bridles off and let them graze while we ate and chatted

(although Emerald was far more interested in my egg and cress sandwich than the grass!). There was no loo, so we had to hold each other's ponies while we went in the bushes! It was so funny having to do that and we couldn't stop giggling. I held Sugar for Madi, and this time Emerald didn't seem to mind standing that close to her – she really is making progress!

We rode a different way back to the yard, and Sally let us all have a canter up this stubble field. It was brilliant! Millie and Tally went bombing off really fast, and only Lydia and Fly overtook them. I would've loved a seriously fast gallop, but I knew it wouldn't be good for Emerald to get that razzed up (I wanted to be sure she'd stop again!), so I tucked her in behind Sugar and Monsoon and had a gentle canter to the top. She really enjoyed it and easily came back to a nice springy trot when I asked.

In fact she did brilliantly the whole way back. We even had to walk through this river, and it wasn't that deep, but she got a bit spooked by the shadows on the water. Instead of panicking, I just stuck closely behind Sally and followed Blue across without even looking down. Before Emerald knew it, we were on the other side.

Oh, and now Jody's calling us in because me and Frankie are on the rota for laying the table and helping get the tea. Better go!

Thursday, just before lights out

Well, I didn't think I could get any prouder of
Emerald after the picnic ride, but I am now!

We had a DVD night tonight, and we
were all watching *Spirit* and eating
popcorn (yum!) when Sally popped
her head round the games room

door and called me over. I was worried for a
minute that I'd done something wrong, but in
fact she wanted me to come up to the field with
her and try turning Emerald out with the other
ponies again. I asked if Frankie could come too,
and Sally said OK, so we all collected Emerald
from the barn and walked up to the field.

The sun was just starting to go down and
everything was glowing golden, and the smell of
grass and dry dirt and Emerald was all around
me. Being out there with my great instructor
and my new friend and my fab pony was just
the best feeling ever, and I had to push away
the thought that tomorrow Pony Camp is
coming to an end.

Sally let me walk Emerald into the field and
take off her lead rope. I gave her a big pat and
whispered in her ear, "Go on, be brave. If *I*
can make new friends, I know you can, too."
Then I gave her mane a final ruffle and walked
away.

I hitched myself up on to the fence with Sally
and Frankie, and we all watched.

At first Emerald just stood there, and I felt a knot in my stomach and a lump in my throat. I so desperately wanted to see her fit in – I just wished I could go and make friends *for* her!

She stood still for a while longer, and then, slowly, she began to wander around the group in a big circle, staying quite a way apart from them. I kept expecting her to bolt at them like she had before, but she didn't (phew!). Instead, she walked in smaller and smaller circles around Flame, Shine and Charm, as the other ponies moved off to graze further away.

She kept circling closer and closer, and I looked to Sally because I was worried she was about to get chased away like last time and maybe even kicked. But Sally smiled at me and said, "Nearly there. Watch."

And then the most amazing thing happened.

Flame kind of shifted so that she was standing sideways to Emerald, and Emerald

went up to her. I held my breath because
I thought the others would definitely
chase her then, but they didn't
seem bothered. Flame nudged
Emerald around a bit and
Emerald just let her, and then
suddenly they were all grazing together and it
looked like Emerald had always belonged there.

I felt all this happiness bubble up inside me,
along with sadness that tomorrow I'll have to
say goodbye to her. Sally squeezed my arm and
said, "Well done, Emily. You helped her to do
that, you know."

"Oh, I—" I began, but Frankie cut me off.

"Yeah, well done, Em, you're like a total horse
whisperer or something!" she said, grinning.

As we walked down the lane, Frankie linked arms with me, and when we got back to the games room, the others were so curious about what we'd been up to that Millie had to pause the DVD so we could tell them all about Emerald joining the others in the field. Well, Frankie, being Frankie, did most of the talking and me, being me, blushed when she told them how Sally said I'd helped Emerald have the confidence to become part of the group.

Then I sat down and Neema put her legs on my lap and Madi asked me to braid her hair. Somehow, I don't think I'll wish I was invisible ever again.

There is one thing I *do* wish, though – I wish that Pony Camp would never end and that I could keep coming to Sunnyside Stables and seeing Emerald for ever and ever!

Friday — back in my new room in our new house. I've got the most AMAZING news!

Well, when I saw Sally talking to Mum while we were getting ready for the gymkhana I had no idea that they were saying anything much. But it turns out that they were saying something v. v. important, which I will reveal in a minute!

First of all, I just want to quickly write about how well Emerald did in the gymkhana. We all spent ages making our ponies look nice for it and cleaning our tack.

When I finished, Emerald looked like this:

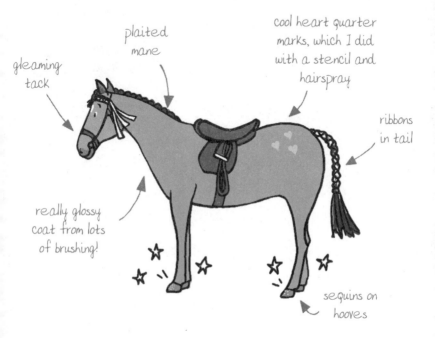

gleaming
tack

plaited
mane

cool heart quarter
marks, which I did
with a stencil and
hairspray

ribbons
in tail

really glossy
coat from lots
of brushing!

sequins on
hooves

It was great to see Mum again. Of course,
she fell totally in love with Emerald, and she was
so surprised at me talking away about our
lessons, and the picnic ride, and Frankie and the
other girls, and Sally and Western Bob, instead
of being quiet like I usually am.

I'd decided with Sally before the gymkhana that I'd join in with Group A's races, but only some of them.

So, me and Emerald did:

Walk, trot, canter

Weaving round the cones

Ball and bucket race

Apple bobbing.

But we missed out the relay and the bale stepping stones races because I thought she'd find those too spooky. I managed to keep her in check during our races, even though it meant that in the apple bobbing I stayed in trot when the others cantered up to the buckets. Amazingly, we actually won the walk, trot, canter against Frankie and Millie – Emerald's speed when I *did* let her go meant we pipped even super-fast Tally at the post!

After both groups had had their gymkhana games, everyone played Chase Me Charlie. Well, all except us. As I hadn't tried any jumping with Emerald, a competition with everyone watching didn't seem like a great place to start, so I led her off into the barn for a rest.

When I got back, I leaned on the fence next to Mum to watch the rest of the jumping. Johnny was in charge with Sally helping, and when she saw me she came over and said well done for handling the gymkhana games.

"Without you, Emerald wouldn't have achieved the amazing things she has done," she said, and I suddenly realized that without *Sally*, me and Emerald wouldn't have achieved anything at all! In fact, we wouldn't even have been together! I said thanks to her for believing in me and giving me the chance to have Emerald as my pony for the week, and for rearranging the lessons for me and getting

Western Bob in to help us and, well, *everything*!
Then I added, "I was worried you were going to
swap me off her, though!"

Sally smiled and said, "I did think about it. But
I felt that you and Emerald were right for each
other. You've taught each other what you
needed to learn most – confidence. Funny how
the things ponies have to teach us are
sometimes not about technique or even about
riding at all!"

I felt a big wave of love for Emerald then,
and after that an even bigger wave of sadness
that I'd have to leave her. I'd pushed it to the
back of my mind so I could enjoy my last day,
but just then the full force of having to say
goodbye hit me and tears sprang into my eyes.
I was just about to rush off to the barn to
spend every single moment I had left at Pony
Camp with her (and probably cry a LOT!),
when Sally said casually, "Oh, it's such a shame,

one of my best term-time helpers has just moved away. The yard's going to be such a mess without her."

I hardly dared to ask in case she said no, but I knew I had to take the chance. "I'd like to volunteer, and I bet Frankie would, too, if you think we'd be good enough," I managed to mumble. I looked up nervously.

"I think you'd both be great!" she said. And I *had* to duck under the fence and give her a hug, even though she's the instructor! Then I looked at Mum and she was beaming – turns out Sally had already cleared it with her (so *that's* what they were talking about!).

For a moment this horrible thought flashed through my head that perhaps there would be older girls helping on the yard as well who'd be horrible to me, but I know it's not like that here.

Then Sally said something even more amazing, which was, "Emerald will need some consistency and won't be suitable as a riding school pony for a long while yet, so if you can ride her every couple of days you'll be helping her, too. And we'll keep working with Western Bob to really get her settled."

I was just absolutely staring at her, grinning. I said thank you loads of times, but even if I'd said it a million times, it wouldn't have seemed like enough. Sally said it was enough after about 23 times, though!

After that, I still wanted Frankie to win the Chase Me Charlie, but I also wanted her to be out straight away so I could tell her the brilliant news! (She came third in the end, after Chantelle and Harry.)

Of course, it was still sad when Pony Camp was over, because us girls won't be together any more. Morgan and Madison were both in

tears about leaving their ponies, so the rest of
us did our best to cheer them up. We got the
mums and dads to take loads of photos of us
all squashed on to the bench, sitting on each
other's laps and stuff. When I remember how
I didn't dare join in with sitting on the bench at
first I can hardly believe it now! Without even
thinking about being shy, I just plonked myself
down on to Chantelle's lap. She was yelling,
"OW, my legs!" and everyone was giggling and
leaning on each other. Mum took a picture of
us on my camera. I haven't downloaded it yet,
but here's my drawing of what we looked like:

I'm seeing Emerald on Tuesday for a one to one session with Sally, but I still said a big goodbye to her, and gave her loads of hugs and kisses and strokes and pats because I'll miss her so much until then. Then I pinned the first place rosette to her bridle so Mum could take a picture of us, and she looked so proud of herself.

Wow, it's amazing how much me and Emerald have helped each other this week, and it's even more amazing that it's only the beginning of our partnership!

I feel like the luckiest girl in the world – I've made a true friend in Frankie and found a lovely stable yard where we can both help out in return for rides, and met a brilliant instructor, but best of all I've teamed up with the most beautiful, wonderful, special pony! I just know it's going to be…

"♡ Em & Em ♡" FOR EVER
x x x

For Austen, with thanks xx

With special thanks to our cover stars,
Maddie and Rusail, pony guru Janet Rising
and our fab photographer, Zoe Cannon.

www.kellymckain.co.uk

STRIPES PUBLISHING
An imprint of Magi Publications
1 The Coda Centre, 189 Munster Road, London SW6 6AW

A paperback original
First published in Great Britain in 2008

Text copyright © Kelly McKain, 2008
Illustrations copyright © Mandy Stanley, 2008
Cover photograph copyright © Zoe Cannon, 2008

ISBN: 978-1-84715-057-8

Printed in Belgium

2 4 6 8 10 9 7 5 3 1